DETECTIVE
NOSEGOODE
and the
KIDNAPPERS

DETECTIVE
NOSEGOODE

and the
KIDNAPPERS

Marian Orłoń

Illustrated by Jerzy Flisak

Translated by Eliza Marciniak

PUSHKIN CHILDREN'S BOOKS

Pushkin Press
71–75 Shelton Street
London, WC2H 9JQ

Original text © Maria Orłoń 2013
Illustrations © Piotr Flisak and Mikołaj Flisak 2013
English translation © Eliza Marciniak 2017

Detective Nosegoode and the Kidnappers was first published as *Detektyw Nosek i porywacze*, 1973

Published by arrangement of Wydawnictwo Dwie Siostry, Warsaw (Poland)

First published by Pushkin Press in 2017

PUBLICATION SUBSIDIZED BY
THE POLISH BOOK INSTITUTE

BOOK INSTITUTE

THE ©POLAND
TRANSLATION
PROGRAM

©POLAND

10 9 8 7 6 5 4 3 2 1

ISBN 13: 978 1 782691 57 0

Designed and typeset by Tetragon, London
Printed and bound by TJ International, Padstow, Cornwall

www.pushkinpress.com

CODY'S BIG DAY

Cody – the strangest of all dogs – was lying in the shade of an apple tree, daydreaming about a big, juicy bone, which his master and friend Detective Ambrosius Nosegoode had gone out to get for him in the centre of town.

"Waiting for a big, juicy bone is the most pleasant kind of waiting," the dog muttered* under his breath, licking his lips expectantly.

The happy wait and the beautiful spring, which had transformed the garden in Skylark Lane into a piece of real paradise, made Cody even dreamier.

---

* Many readers might be surprised at this and might point out that Cody couldn't have muttered these words because dogs do not mutter. Indeed, as a rule, dogs don't know human speech – but Cody is an exception to this rule and can use our language perfectly. You can find out how this happened and read about the earlier adventures of Mr Nosegoode and his dog in *Detective Nosegoode and the Music Box Mystery*.

This dog's life is so good, he thought. *Other dogs go hungry in rickety kennels and are used to the smack of a stick or the clutch of a tight collar, while I have a good friend, a quiet corner to enjoy in my old age and, once in a while, a tasty bone for dessert. What else could I ask for?*

The familiar creak of the front gate interrupted this enjoyable train of thought.

"Ambrosius!" Cody yelped in delight and ran to greet his friend.

His joy quickly faded. One glance was enough for him to realize that Ambrosius had returned without a bone. He was carrying a parcel, but the flat, rectangular bundle couldn't possibly contain such a delicacy. Cody glumly hung his tail, and life suddenly seemed a bitter pill to swallow. He sighed.

Ambrosius, who heard the sigh, smiled mysteriously, jiggled the package and said, "I promise you a ton of bones if you guess what's inside."

"Thanks a lot," Cody barked back, "but I'd rather have one bone between my teeth than a ton at the butcher's. Besides, I have no interest in mysterious bundles."

"Really?" Ambrosius bent down towards him. "I'm sure you're going to change your mind very soon."

Cody assumed a dignified posture.

"Don't forget that I'm not the kind of dog who changes his mind," he said emphatically.

"We'll see."

Mr Nosegoode quickly removed the wrapping and showed his dog a beautiful book which still smelled of fresh printers' ink.

"Look!"

Cody glanced at the title and leapt up onto all fours.

"*Portraits of Extraordinary Dogs?!*" he exclaimed.

"Indeed!" Ambrosius said, pleased that the book made such an impression. "The volume in front of you is Timothy Pipestem's epoch-making work."

Cody instantly forgot about such mundane things as big, juicy bones. The events from a year earlier came flooding back to him vividly. It had all begun when a mysterious stranger with a beard appeared in Lower Limewood. From the first day, the stranger seemed unduly interested in Cody: he watched him closely, he followed him... Cody began to suspect terrible things. He took the bearded man for a dangerous criminal, a poisoner even. But then it turned out that he was a great friend of dogs.

This stranger was Timothy Pipestem – a well-respected dog expert who travelled from town to town gathering material for his book – the very book that Mr Nosegoode was now holding in his hands.

"Ambrosius," Cody whispered, shifting anxiously from paw to paw. "Do I... Do I get a mention in there?"

"A mention?" the detective said indignantly. "Just a mention? Timothy Pipestem has devoted one hundred and forty-eight complimentary words to you, accompanied by a photograph."

Ambrosius flipped a few pages and showed Cody the photo.

"Look, here you are!"

Cody gaped at the portrait, momentarily forgetting everything around him. He found it difficult to accept that this fascinating dog looking out at him from the book was none other than himself.

"So, how do you like it?" Ambrosius asked.

Cody swallowed.

"Not bad!"

"Not bad? It's brilliant! Look at that sparkle in your eye, the placement of your tail, the positioning of your ears, the intelligence evident in the muzzle... Timothy Pipestem has captured the essence of your dogly being – and all you can say is, "'Not bad'..."

Cody listened to this reproach with a guilty expression, inwardly admitting that his friend was absolutely right.

"Now listen to what our excellent cynologist* has written about you," Ambrosius continued. "Or maybe you'd rather read it out yourself?"

---

* A cynologist is a specialist in the study of dogs.

"No, no!" the dog answered quickly. "You read. I've got something in my eye; I can hardly see."

He didn't want to admit that emotion was squeezing his throat like a tight collar and that the letters were dancing in front of his eyes.

Ambrosius cleared his throat and began to read.

Here is another eminent representative of the canine family – Cody, who belongs to retired Detective Ambrosius Nosegoode (7 Skylark Lane, Lower Limewood). Cody seems like an ordinary mutt, but his outstanding intelligence places him among dogs of the most noble birth. Mr Nosegoode's professional successes are well known. It should be noted, however, without detracting in any way from the famous detective's talents, that the phenomenal Cody has been jointly responsible for many of them. And that's not all. Certain facts seem to point to Cody possessing an ability that has never been found in animals up to now. This ability is so incredible that the author – keen to maintain the scientific accuracy of this work – has decided not to reveal it. Let it be noted that if this ability were to be confirmed, it would undoubtedly mean that Cody is the most brilliant dog in the world.

Ambrosius finished reading and slowly closed the book. "Yes, my friend!" he said. "From this day on, you can hold your tail high. You're now the most famous dog in the world. This makes me very happy, but it also worries me."

"It worries you?" Cody said, surprised. The excerpt from the book had made him feel a bit light-headed. "Why?"

The old detective stared at a butterfly fluttering above his head. After a pause, without taking his eyes off it, he said, "I'm afraid of losing you."

"Ambrosius, what on earth are you talking about?" Cody blurted out.

"I know what I'm saying," the detective stood his ground. "'The most brilliant dog in the world' – that's not the same as the little-known Cody. It's true that Timothy Pipestem hasn't actually said that you can talk, but you'll get all kinds of proposals regardless. You'll see, you'll soon get offers to join a circus or be in a show! And popularity, fame, applause – these are enormous temptations. Who knows, they might persuade you. Old Ambrosius can't offer you much any more..."

The dog grew serious.

"Get this into your head once and for all: I'm never going to leave you," he assured him eagerly. "Never! Not for all the circuses in the world! Do you believe me?"

Ambrosius didn't answer. He just laid his hand on the dog's back and remained like that for a while, moved by his friend's words. He had no idea that an entirely different kind of danger was looming over the house in Skylark Lane...

THE
MYSTERIOUS LETTER

Nearly every day for a week, the postman had stopped in front of Mr Nosegoode's house to take out an unusual number of envelopes from his bulging bag. They were letters from the numerous friends of the old detective and his dog who had bought a copy of *Portraits of Extraordinary Dogs* and hastened to express their congratulations and best wishes.

Ambrosius got so used to these tokens of friendship that when he saw the postman standing in front of the gate that Wednesday he had no doubts as to what was in his bag.

"More congratulations!" he called out to Cody. "I'll go outside to save the postman a few steps."

He shuffled out to the front gate, took the envelope and came back inside, examining it closely, as he always did.

"I have a feeling this one isn't congratulations," he said, turning the letter over in his hands.

"Why do you say that?" the dog asked with surprise.

Ambrosius showed him the envelope.

"Have a good look, and you'll see what I mean."

The dog stared at the envelope, sniffed it and gave his master a puzzled look.

"I don't see anything interesting. It smells of Seven Flowers soap... but what can you tell from that?"

"You're right, it's hard to tell anything about the contents of the letter from the smell of Seven Flowers," Ambrosius agreed, "but smell isn't everything. You've missed the most important detail."

"Meaning?" the dog asked in an offended tone.

"Look at the address."

Cody craned his neck and slowly read out loud, "'To dedective Ambrozius Nosegood...'"

"And?"

The dog scratched his left ear.

"Hmm... It sounds too official for a note of congratulations. You're right."

"Too official and too incorrect," Ambrosius pointed out. "None of our friends would have made such errors."

"Errors?" Cody asked, feeling a bit embarrassed. He regarded spelling as one of the most incomprehensible of human inventions and could not for the life of him understand why a stake in the ground was spelt differently from the steak he liked to eat.

Ambrosius nodded.

"That's right, my friend, errors! Nobody who personally knows and likes Detective Ambrosius Nosegoode would ever write 'dedective' or 'Ambrozius Nosegood', but that's just what we have here, which is why this letter really intrigues me."

Cody licked his lips, as if he'd smelled a tasty treat, and said, "So open it! What are we waiting for?"

"I was just about to," Ambrosius replied and carefully tore open the envelope.

Mr Nosegood!
We have something
important to tell
discus with you. If
you want to know
what it is, come

The piece of paper he pulled out had been torn from a school notebook. The author of the letter couldn't have been very concerned about its appearance. Ragged edges and a large stain near the bottom of the page made a bad first impression, which was made worse by the uneven, clumsy letters and numerous crossings-out in the text. Evidently, the author didn't care what the reader was going to think of his correspondent.

Ambrosius scanned the page and whistled to himself.

"Anything interesting?" Cody couldn't bear the suspense any longer.

"Very interesting! Listen to this."

The dog shifted his weight from paw to paw and raised his head as the detective began reading.

> *13 May*
>
> *Mr Nosegood!*
> *We have something important to ~~tell~~ discus with you. If you want to know what it is, come to Birch Grove on ~~Wednesday~~ Thursday evning at ten oclock. You have to come alone. If you bring somebody, you wont learn anything. Don't tell anybody about the ~~apoint~~ meeting. We mite be late, so wait for half an hour.*   *Two Guys*

*

As his friend read out the letter, Cody's whole manner changed. He first looked curious, then anxious, and then scared – very scared. When Ambrosius lifted his eyes from the page, the dog was sitting paralysed with fear.

"So, what do you think?" said the detective, who was the first to speak.

"It's... it's some kind of trick," Cody stammered out. "They're up to no good. You're not going to go, are you?"

"Oh, I definitely feel like going," Ambrosius replied.

The carefree way in which he said these words made Cody very distressed.

"How can you say that!" he cried out. "Can't you sense the danger? Do you think that those 'two guys' are trying to get you to meet them in that secluded place so that you can listen to nightingales together? Or gaze at the moon?"

"Oh no, I don't suppose they have such romantic hobbies," Ambrosius continued light-heartedly. "But I'm not particularly afraid."

The dog was beside himself.

"Ha, look at him! "Oh, I'm not afraid!" The fearless detective Ambrosius Nosegoode triumphs over two dangerous criminals," he continued ironically. "Is fame really more important to you than your own life?"

"Both are important to me," came the calm reply. "But I'm not afraid because the author of the letter doesn't seem to be particularly bright."

"So you've guessed who it might be?" Cody asked.

"Not at all! But it's hard to consider someone bright if they've made seven serious spelling mistakes in such a short letter, not counting those on the envelope. I think I can handle such an opponent. That's why I'm going to go to this meeting."

Cody quickly turned meek. All desire to argue left him. He realized that he wasn't going to get anywhere by shouting.

He looked imploringly at his friend and said, "Please don't do it, Ambrosius! But if you must go, take me with you. I can keep a lookout for you."

Ambrosius hesitated for a moment and then shook his head.

"No. If I'm going, I'll go alone. You see, I like fair play." Seeing the troubled look on his friend's face, he added casually, "Come on, old boy! Tail up! Tomorrow you'll be laughing about these misgivings, you'll see!"

"I'd like to," the dog replied quietly. "I'd very much like to be laughing tomorrow..."

CODY, WHERE ARE YOU?

It was a clear, warm evening. The sky was studded with stars, and grasshoppers were chirping merrily in the fields all around. There wasn't a soul in sight, although the tousled willows along the road leading from Lower Limewood to Birch Grove looked like witches lying in wait for unsuspecting victims.

Ambrosius came to a stop next to one of the willows. He turned around to face the town, whose lights twinkled in the distance, and listened intently. There were no sounds coming from that direction. There was only unbroken silence: not a single suspicious noise or rustle... *So he stayed home.* Ambrosius breathed a sigh of relief. *He listened to me after all!*

Up until this point, he hadn't been sure that Cody wasn't following him. It was true that the dog had declared, in a voice full of hurt pride, that he wasn't going to go where he wasn't wanted, but that might have been a ploy to make Ambrosius less watchful. That's why the detective kept listening closely for Cody creeping behind him and paused every now and then to see if he could make out the familiar figure in the dark. But Cody hadn't followed him – he was certain of that now.

It's good that he listened to me, Ambrosius told himself, but in his heart of hearts he had to admit that he would've felt more at ease in the company of his trusted friend. His cane and the big cap pistol which weighed down his pocket would be no substitutes for Cody in case of danger. On many occasions, Cody had shown great presence of mind and exceptional courage. This time, however, he had to stay home. It couldn't be helped. Fair play was a sacred thing – even if one's opponent was a criminal. Or at least that was one of Mr Nosegoode's principles, and all the criminals he had ever pursued knew it well. They knew it, and they respected him for it.

A few hundred steps still separated Ambrosius from the trees of Birch Grove. They were there ahead of him like a black, impenetrable wall. What mysteries did the grove hide? Who was lurking in the undergrowth? Why did they pick such a secluded spot for a meeting? What would they demand? All these questions awaited answers.

Ambrosius looked at his watch: it was five to ten.

"I have to hurry!" he muttered. "Punctuality is the politeness not just of kings but also of detectives."

He glanced once more at the lights of Lower Limewood, listened intently one more time and then resumed his steps.

Outwardly, he gave the impression of walking casually, as if he were out for a stroll or going shopping, but in reality he was tense and focused, straining his ears and eyes to the utmost. After all, every willow, every bush, every roadside boulder could be hiding a surprise, and he needed to be ready.

But there were no surprises, and a few minutes later Ambrosius reached the edge of the grove. He was greeted by a gentle rustle of leaves and the flutter of a bird scared away by this late, unexpected visitor. He looked around uncertainly, waited a while and then cleared his throat a couple of times.

When nothing happened, he called out, "Hello, is there anybody there?"

There was no answer – only silence. Ambrosius shrugged and looked at his watch. It was two minutes past ten o'clock. He remembered the letter: *We might be late, so wait for half an hour.*

It was nice of them to forewarn me, he thought, *but I'd rather be dealing with punctual people.* He took his pipe out of his pocket and put it in his mouth. *Or maybe they're somewhere close by?* he thought. *Maybe they're watching me from their hiding place, waiting for the right moment to show themselves. If that's the case, let them watch. By all means! I'm going to sit on this stump and wait. They'd better not be long though. It's a beautiful night, no doubt about it, but sleep is important too. And in any case, I don't want Cody to worry.*

He sat perched on top of the stump, leant his head on his cane and was soon lost in thought. He recalled the old days, the various cases he'd solved... Capturing the Elusive Hand, unmasking the Chess Club burglar, tricking the art thieves at the museum. Those were wonderful times! In those days, every schoolchild knew the name of Ambrosius Nosegoode, and photographs of him often graced the front pages of the most widely read dailies. And now? Retirement. Although...

Ambrosius suddenly remembered where he was. Engrossed in his memories, he had completely lost track of time. He peered anxiously at his watch. Ten thirty-five! So they hadn't come! But why? All sorts of thoughts flashed through his mind. Maybe something unforeseen had happened? Maybe somebody had found out about the planned meeting and decided to prevent it? Or maybe it had all been a bad joke played on him by some rascal? Or maybe... A shiver of terror ran down his spine. How could he not have thought of it before! How could he have been so careless! Why did he?...

Without another thought, he leapt up from the stump, gripped his cane tightly and started running towards the town as fast as he could. The words from the letter rang in his ears: *If you bring somebody, you won't learn anything.* This sentence made him hurry twice as fast. He sprinted without paying attention to the bumps in the ground or to his own rapid heartbeat. *I just hope I make it in time!* he thought. *I have to make it!* At last he reached the first houses on the outskirts of Lower Limewood. He didn't slow down despite the fact that the stamping of his feet on the pavement sounded like an alarm through the sleeping town.

Then at last he was in Skylark Lane. Number one... two... three... Only a few dozen steps left – and here was number seven!

Ambrosius halted, wiped the sweat off his forehead, caught his breath and anxiously – very anxiously – pressed the handle on the front gate. It opened easily. But that in itself didn't mean anything, since he hadn't locked it on his way out.

Trying to stop his voice from trembling, he called out in the direction of the house, "Cody! Cody, where are you?"

He waited hopefully for a few seconds, but when there was no answer – when Cody didn't run out to meet him, didn't come to rub himself against his legs, didn't greet him with a joyful bark – Ambrosius realized that the worst had happened. Cody had been kidnapped!

"They've managed to outwit me!" he groaned. "They've made a fool of me!"

The bitterness of defeat overwhelmed him for only a moment. He quickly shook it off and added grimly, "But the fun isn't over yet! The game's only just begun!"

IN THE HANDS OF
THE KIDNAPPERS

The door closed with a piercing creak and Cody was left alone. The first thing he saw in the darkness was a little barred window, with a small rectangle of dark-blue sky and a few stars beyond. Some time passed before he got used to the gloom and realized that he was in a small, cluttered room, which smelled of old junk and mice. He cautiously reached out a paw and felt a musty sack lying on the floor. He crouched on top of it and perked up his ears, trying to hear what his captors were talking about in the adjacent room. But their conversation turned out to be uninteresting: they were simply getting ready to leave their hideout. Indeed, a moment later, the voices grew more distant, a bolt clanked into place and everything fell silent. The dog remained in the same position for a while, listening, before sinking down onto the sack. Once more, this time calmly, he began going over the surprising events of the last hour or so.

To begin with, Ambrosius had left. It was exactly nine thirty-five. Cody accompanied him to the front gate, warned him again to be careful and then lay down in front of the house to wait for his friend's return. He was worried, of course, but the light-hearted manner with which Ambrosius was treating the whole affair made him feel a bit better. He even managed to nod off for about fifteen minutes.

Cody was woken by ten resounding strikes of the clock on the town hall tower. He blinked a few times and yawned, feeling guilty that he'd given in to sleep instead of keeping watch. Just then, he heard footsteps on the pavement – quick, loud footsteps approaching the gate. He felt a sense of foreboding. He leapt up onto all fours and waited. He guessed – no, he was certain now – that these footsteps heralded misfortune. That's why he wasn't surprised when the gate swung open and a young stranger burst into the yard. When he saw the dog, the stranger stopped and looked a bit unsure of himself. Then he began to speak, trying to make his voice sound as gentle as possible.

"Something bad has happened, little doggy. Your master is in danger. He needs your help. We have to go to him, straight away. You're going to come with me, right? Good doggy, you're going to come..."

How difficult it was for Cody to hold his tongue! He wanted to ask what danger Ambrosius was in, where they could find him and whether they'd make it in time. But instead of these questions, he only barked in agreement and followed the outstretched hand, in which a tasty ring of smoked sausage had appeared out of nowhere. Cody seemed not to notice the sausage at all, preoccupied as he was by a single thought: Ambrosius was in danger!

They hurried through Lower Limewood's deserted streets and within minutes were past the last houses. Cody found it a bit odd that instead of going west, towards Birch Grove, they headed north. *Maybe Ambrosius has been abducted,* he thought. *Or maybe at the last minute he was told to go somewhere else.*

They left the main road for an unpaved track leading to the Old Mill. *Is that where we're going?* The dog was surprised. He knew the old ruin. It stood in the middle of a farm field three miles out of town, and there were stories that it was haunted by the miller's ghost. The ghost would appear at midnight and start turning the sails of the windmill, which hadn't been used for many years. Is that where Ambrosius was being held? *Ah, if only I could smell things as well as I used to!* Cody sighed. *I could find him without anyone's help!*

The journey seemed unbearably long. Cody's companion tried to entertain him with tales of a sumptuous supper which awaited them but, in the circumstances, this usually pleasant thought held no interest for Cody at all.

Feeling tired, they finally reached their goal. In front of them was a dark, gloomy building that showed no signs of life. Only the outstretched sails seemed to say, "Stop – you've arrived!" Cody was so tense he was shaking, but his guide remained amazingly calm. He turned to Cody as if nothing was happening, beckoned to him with the hand in which he still held the sausage and began climbing the creaky wooden steps at the front of the mill. The steps led to a door some way above the ground. Cody's companion fiddled with something, pushed the door and disappeared in the dark opening. The dog slipped in noiselessly behind him. As soon as he was inside, the door quickly closed, and Cody was plunged into total darkness. Then a match was struck, a candle spluttered and a wobbly flame illuminated dangling ropes, huge cogwheels and a pair of enormous millstones. The young stranger set the candle down on top of the millstones. Cody automatically followed it with his eyes... and he almost had to sit down! There on the stone lay a copy of *Portraits of Extraordinary Dogs*!!!

So that's what this is all about! he suddenly realized. *They weren't after Ambrosius at all; they were after me! The whole goal of this treacherous plan was to lure me here!*

Cody was furious. He examined the young stranger more closely. He was a tall, skinny boy, with a face covered in spots. He didn't look very likeable. Cody had the urge to jump on him, bite his calf and force him to open the door. He might've even done it, if it hadn't been for the sound of heavy footsteps on the stairs. *That must be the second guy,* he guessed. *It's worth taking a look at him.* As he predicted, the door swung open and Spotty's pal burst inside. In stark contrast to his friend, he was short and plump, like a barrel. He slammed the door shut and gasped, "At last! How did it go?"

"He came along without a fuss, like he was under a spell. He must really love smoked sausages. What about the old man?"

Barrel sniggered.

"He trudged off to Birch Grove. I hid behind the fire station and watched him walk off into the fields. I waited a while and ran over here. I'd love to see his face when he gets home."

"Me too," Spotty said.

I bet you're going to see it soon! the dog wanted to shout. *But I doubt you're going to be so jolly then!* Wishing them a prompt encounter with Ambrosius, he pondered what to do next. He could escape, of course, but would that be the best solution? Maybe it would be better to play the role of a dumb animal who's interested in nothing but sausages. He could eavesdrop on their conversation, find out their plans and make sure they couldn't carry them out. Because they had to have plans for him – otherwise they wouldn't have kidnapped him.

Deciding that this was the best course of action, Cody barked hopefully, pointing to the sausage with his nose. The two boys were amused.

"See how smart he is?" Spotty was pleased, offering him a piece. "I think what's-his-name, Pipestem or whatever, was right when he said this was an exceptional dog."

"If my aunt hadn't bought that book," Barrel pointed to the copy of *Portraits*, "we'd never have found out about him."

"Your aunt has been invaluable," Spotty admitted. "If it all goes according to plan, we should buy her a present – maybe a new nightcap to doze off in!" he said with a laugh. He quickly grew serious again and added, "You haven't let it slip that we've borrowed the book, right?"

Barrel was offended.

"Come on, what do you take me for?"

They turned their attention back to the dog, who appeared to care for nothing in the world except his food. In fact, he was doing his best not to miss a single word of their conversation.

"So, what do you think, what's this extraordinary ability of his?" Barrel asked. "According to Pipestem's book it's something really incredible."

"Nonsense!" Spotty replied sneeringly. "He's got no extraordinary abilities. He's just smart and well trained, like a police dog, that's all. Anyway, that's all we need."

Barrel wasn't convinced.

"Maybe he can count or dance?"

"Maybe. I once heard about a dog who knew all his times tables by heart."

"All of it?" Barrel said doubtfully, since he hadn't yet managed to master that trick himself.

"Yeah, all of it."

Barrel looked at the dog with reverence. Maybe this one also had it memorized.

"Go on, ask him what's two times two!" Spotty egged his friend on.

But Barrel, detecting mockery in Spotty's voice, quickly changed the subject.

"How about you tell me when we're going to start practising," he said.

"In a few days. We have to wait until the dog gets used to us."

"What if he runs off?"

"He won't run off. We'll bribe him with doggy treats. You'll see how attached to us he's going to get!"

"But that's going to cost us..."

"So what? We'll make up for it later. There's a heap of dosh coming our way, my friend!" His voice became dreamy.

"That's all down to him," Barrel said after a pause, looking at the dog.

"That's why we need to take good care of him. He's already had his supper, and now it's time for sleep."

"Where are we going to keep him? In here?" Barrel asked, looking around the room.

"No. In the storeroom. It's safer."

"Well, get him in there then. It's time we got going!"

Spotty nodded and stepped towards the dog.

"Nice doggy," he said. "Come to your room and have a lie-down..."

He stroked Cody's back and pointed him towards a little door leading deeper into the mill. Not wanting to arouse suspicion, Cody wagged his tail amiably – even though it was one of the most difficult things he'd ever done in his life. Spotty, touched by the gesture, patted him on the back again, opened the door and gently pushed him inside.

*

Lying in the dim storeroom, Cody is racking his brains about what to do. It's pretty clear that Spotty and Barrel are planning to commit a crime of some sort, and that he – Cody – is supposed to play a key part in it. How should he behave in this situation? Should he run away at the first chance he gets? Or should he allow them to keep plotting, get to know all their plans and then unmask them when the time comes?

*

Cody thought for quite a while before settling on the second option. *I'll stay here!* he decided. *But I have to let Ambrosius know where I am, or he's going to worry. I have to tell him I'm alive and well. But how? How can I get touch with him?*

This vexing question kept him awake very late into the night.

THE FIRST CLUES

Ambrosius finally managed to fall asleep around dawn but woke up an hour later with the vague sense that something bad had happened. He couldn't remember what it was. Only when he was fully awake did he recall the events of the previous day, and anxiety about his friend fell on him like a heavy weight. For a brief moment, he was filled with the hope that he'd soon hear the familiar barking from behind the door; he even listened for it, but the whole house was silent. The only sounds he could hear came from the outside, through the open window: the chirping of birds and the clatter of a cart rolling over the cobblestones.

Ambrosius briskly jumped out of bed and started preparing a plan of action as he went about his morning routine.

I'll interview the neighbours first, he decided. *I'll start with Mrs Hardtack, whose eyes and ears can always be relied on. Then I'll need to talk to Constable Longbeak, who was on duty last night and who might've noticed something. Finally, I'll have to look at the letter from the "Two Guys" again. I didn't pay enough attention to it yesterday, but that piece of paper is the kidnappers' calling card. They must've left some clues on it.* Absorbed in these thoughts and with his spirits lifted a little, he walked over to Mrs Hardtack's. He was glad to see her in front of her house, feeding her hen, the wonderfully named Hortensia. She seemed pleasantly surprised by her neighbour's early visit.

"I see you're up even before my Hortensia, Mr Nosegoode!" she greeted him. "How can you get up so early?"

Smiling winningly, Mr Nosegoode replied that it clearly couldn't be a serious a crime since his charming neighbour was also guilty of it, and then he asked her what time she had gone to bed.

Mrs Hardtack, who was well known for being very talkative, was momentarily speechless. Then she asked, with a touch of sarcasm in her voice, "Would you also like to know if I slept on my left side or my right, Inspector?"

Bowing humbly to express regret that his curiosity had been misunderstood, Ambrosius wondered how to justify his nosiness. If there was one thing he certainly didn't want to do, it was to tell his neighbour about the events of the previous night. In his head, he could hear the wise advice of Hippolytus Whiskers, his old teacher and friend: "If only two extra people know about a crime," the great detective used to say, "that's good. If there's only one person, that's very good. If there are none, that's perfect."

Ambrosius was a firm believer in this principle. He looked at Mrs Hardtack apologetically and explained that he had reason to believe that there had been criminals in the area the previous night around ten o'clock. That was why he had asked such an indelicate question.

"If you were still up at that time," he continued, "you might've heard some suspicious sounds or people talking... I'd be very interested to know, for example, if you heard a car engine."

Mrs Hardtack went pale, put a hand on her chest, leant on the fence and whispered, "Fire and brimstone! Did something happen?"

Mr Nosegoode's calm expression reassured her a bit, and his words did the rest.

"There's absolutely nothing for you to worry about," he replied truthfully. "But if you could answer a few questions..."

"Of course!" she nodded eagerly. "I'll answer your questions, but I don't have much to say. I did go to bed quite late, around half past ten, but I didn't hear anything suspicious. There was no car nearby, that's for sure."

Ambrosius gave her a surprised look, and she added, "You see, my Hortensia here can't stand cars because she was nearly run over once. Since then, whenever she hears the sound of a car engine, she makes an absolute racket. And last night she didn't so much as cluck once. I might've missed a car, but her – never!"

This explanation completely convinced the old detective. He thanked Mrs Hardtack for the information and left to continue his enquiries. He talked to three other neighbours and to Constable Longbeak, but he didn't learn anything that could help him find Cody. The only detail he confirmed was that there'd been no unfamiliar cars in Lower Limewood the night before.

So he went home and, armed with a powerful magnifying glass, began to study the kidnappers' letter. *This is my only hope*, he thought. He carefully examined the smudged postmark on the stamp. He hadn't been wrong when he'd first looked at the envelope. The letter had been posted on the 15th of May in Yeanling, about twelves miles from Lower Limewood.

"An inept attempt to send me on a wild goose chase," Ambrosius muttered to himself. "If the Two Guys live in Yeanling, then I'm an honorary citizen of the Kingdom of Flying Pigs... Cody isn't some dumb animal: he's not going to let himself be dragged on a rope for twelve miles! If they had a car, that would be a different story. But they didn't. Besides, the date... The letter was written on the 13th, but it wasn't posted until the 15th. If someone writes a letter – an important letter! – and carries it around for so long, it's clear they don't want to put it in the nearest postbox – they must be waiting for an opportunity to send it from a different location. It's obvious that I shouldn't look for the kidnappers in Yeanling but somewhere closer. Much closer!"

Mr Nosegoode rubbed his hands. A ray of light at last! Encouraged by his first discovery, he turned his attention to the large stain at the bottom of the page. He looked at it closely, touched it, smelled it and smiled knowingly to himself. Varnish! Yes, it was varnish – and varnish wasn't like water: not everyone had regular dealings with it. So here was another clue!

A few minutes later, the detective's sharp eyes fell on the third clue: the capital letters G and W, each of which appeared twice in the text. Both stood out markedly from the other letters, which were crooked and clumsy. These two had been written with confidence and flair, and they even had little decorative flourishes... It was clear that the author was used to writing them – perhaps had even practised writing them to make them look as good as possible. No extraordinary investigative talent was needed to work out what that meant. There was only one explanation: the letters G and W were the initials of the person who had kidnapped Cody!

Ambrosius's face lit up with satisfaction.

"Getting warmer... getting warmer..." he said to himself, putting the letter back in its envelope.

STRANGE GAMES

The small rectangle of sky that Cody could see through the barred window, and which only a short time earlier had been the colour of a ripe orange, was now dark, and the darkness was deepening with every passing minute. Cody watched it change, fanning himself nervously with his tail.

"Sunday is coming to an end," he muttered. "A third day of horrible boredom. Let's hope it's the last!"

In truth, if it hadn't been for the boredom and his worry about Ambrosius, whom he hadn't been able to inform about his plight, Cody would not have felt too bad. His bedding in the storeroom had turned out to be tolerable, Spotty and Barrel had very good manners, and his meals appeared with an amazing regularity. Admittedly, not all of them were worthy of the Golden Frying Pan award, but it would've been ungrateful to complain.

But the boredom...

Yet this was the day when something was finally going to change. "We'll start tonight," Spotty had said to Barrel that morning with a mysterious look on his face. The memory of this one sentence made Cody await the Two Guys with impatience.

They should be here by now, he thought. He wrinkled his nose. *It'll soon be dark. And I'm hungry…*

Another fifteen minutes passed, however, before he heard a bicycle bell – a sign that they'd arrived.

Annoyed by their lateness, Cody decided to greet them coolly, but the smell of bacon and eggs coming out of the small pot which Spotty and Barrel had brought with them completely ruined his resolve. Cody knew that pot well, and a moment later he was greedily devouring its contents. It didn't take him long because the portion was stingy and he was ravenous. *A miniature pinscher on a diet might be happy enough with this*, he thought, licking out the remains of the meal, *but not me*. When he was done, he looked reproachfully at the two boys, to make it clear that they should do better in the future.

They must have understood him correctly, because Spotty said, "He hasn't had enough. But if he does well today, he's going to get a reward."

So they haven't changed their minds! Cody thought, pleased. *Something is finally going to start happening!*

But his enthusiasm was dampened almost instantly, when he saw that Spotty was holding an object which fills every self-respecting dog with loathing: a collar! Smiling craftily, Spotty moved towards him with the detested symbol of slavery in his hand. Cody took a step back. He wanted to growl, to protest – but he remembered in time that if he wanted to carry out his plan to the end, he had to endure this humiliation. He let Spotty put the offending item around his neck, tie a piece of cord to it and lead him outside.

Out in the fresh air, Cody was able to briefly forget about the collar. It was an enchanting May evening. The time he had spent in the storeroom made the world seem more beautiful to him, as though everything had been refreshed. He stood still, listening to the tinkling of the stars and greedily inhaling the smell of the earth... After a while, he stretched out his neck and gazed at the lights of Lower Limewood flickering on the horizon. One of them belonged to a little house in Skylark Lane. Which one was it? He closed his eyes and saw the cosy interior, the old lamp on top of the chest of drawers, his own bedding in the corner of the room...

What is Ambrosius doing just at this moment? he wondered. *Maybe he's eating his supper, alone? Or maybe he's standing by the window, watching out for my return?*

At these thoughts, he felt a twinge of uncontrollable long-ing to be with his friend. He had to practise great self-control in order not to break free and start running towards those distant lights.

A sharp tug on the cord brought him back to reality.

"Let's go!" Spotty said, and pulled him towards a solitary poplar tree standing in the middle of the farm field a few hundred yards from the mill.

Cody was terribly curious about the purpose of the outing, but not a single word was said about it on the way. It was only when they were standing next to the poplar that Barrel asked, "Have you brought the package?"

"What do you think?" Spotty replied, pulling out a small bundle from inside his shirt.

"What's in it?"

Spotty smiled slyly.

"A reward for the dog."

"Bones?"

"No. Pigeon thighs, my friend!"

Cody could feel his mouth water.

"Well, let's get started!" Barrel prompted.

"Wait!" Spotty held him back and took a good look around to make sure they were alone. Then he laid the bundle down at the foot of the tree and turned to Cody.

"Find it, Cody. Find it!"

Cody struggled with himself. On the one hand, he didn't want to give himself away and show that he instantly understood what was being asked of him; on the other, he had no intention of giving up the reward. He looked uncertainly at Spotty. When the command was repeated, he lowered his head and began sniffing around the tree. At last, he picked up the bundle in his teeth.

"You see!" Spotty exclaimed. He patted the dog, thought for a second and said to Barrel, "Now take a few steps back and call him!"

"You want to let him off the lead?" Barrel was alarmed. "What if he runs off?"

"I have faith in the smell of pigeon thighs!" Spotty reassured him. "No sensible dog would give up such a delicacy. And anyway, we have to start at some point."

"Fine. Let's do it!"

Barrel walked away from the poplar and called the dog. Spotty let go of the cord. There was a tense pause – and Cody raced off towards Barrel.

"Not bad!" Spotty announced approvingly. "Let's see how he does with the next one."

He ordered the dog to come to him, took the bundle out of his mouth and laid it in the same place as before, under the poplar tree.

"Sit!" he commanded.

Cody obeyed the order. Spotty gestured for him to stay while he himself walked over to where Barrel was standing.

He seemed quite nervous, wiping his forehead with the back of his hand. Then he shouted, "Fetch the package, Cody!"

Well, well! Cody perked up. *This game is getting more and more interesting. But what's he driving at? Hang on a minute... I think it's just dawned on me... Yes, that must be it! Ha, not on your life! We can have a bit of fun, but...*

He lifted his head and stared at Spotty mockingly. The boy looked impatient.

"Fetch the package!" he repeated.

Just a moment! Cody reassured him inwardly. *Don't get all worked up! I can't seem too smart.*

The kidnappers exchanged disappointed glances.

"He doesn't understand," Barrel said. "You need to show him what to do."

"I know," Spotty agreed reluctantly and walked back to the tree.

He leaned down, picked up the bundle off the ground and put it right under Cody's nose.

"Take it!"

Cody snapped his teeth and took hold of the package.

"Stay here!" Spotty ordered and went back to stand next to Barrel.

"Fetch the package, Cody!"

Fine, now I can obey, the dog told himself and dashed off towards Spotty and Barrel. He thought he would be finished for the day and that it must be time for his reward, but he was wrong. One more test awaited him – the most important. The kidnappers exchanged a few whispered remarks and then started acting very solemnly, as if they were about to take part in a coronation.

"Hold back the dog!" Spotty said in the voice of a chamberlain.

"I've got him," Barrel replied, picking up the cord.

After pausing to be sure that Barrel had a tight grip on the lead, Spotty set off towards the poplar with stately steps. He laid the bundle of pigeon thighs under the tree, cast a glance over the surrounding fields again and walked

back, in the same dignified manner, to where the dog and his companion were standing.

"Now do it all by yourself! Go to the tree and fetch the package. Go!" He pushed the dog forward gently.

This time, Cody, who was getting bored with the whole game, turned out to be far smarter than the kidnappers had expected. He sprang up, got to the poplar in no time, grabbed the bundle in his teeth and after a few leaps was back beside Spotty and Barrel.

Both of them were so impressed that they were completely dumbstruck. They looked at Cody with genuine admiration. When they recovered, Spotty reached for the package, tore the wrapping paper open and with a gesture full of respect handed Cody two delicious-smelling pigeon thighs.

"Eat!" he said. "You've earned it. You've done so well you deserve a medal!"

Cody glared in his direction with one eye as if to say, "Isn't it too early for a medal?" Then he turned his attention to the reward.

Munching on the delicate bones, he thought, *Go ahead, admire me! As a matter of fact, you'll soon find out how much more I'm capable of, but I have a feeling you won't be so pleased when you do. Yes, my dear kidnappers! You've forgotten that I've spent many years in the service of the great Detective Nosegoode! You've forgotten – and this will be your undoing!*

THE GREEN NOTEBOOK

Even Mr Nosegoode, with his enquiring mind, couldn't work out why none of the town's carpenters had their workshops in Carpenter Street, despite the fact that Lower Limewood had a street with that name. One of these masters of the plane and chisel had chosen Basket Lane, another had set up shop in Swan Way, and the third was based in Barrel-Organ Street.

Mr Nosegoode stopped in front of the first of these workshops and looked up at the large sign over the entrance. While reading the colourful lettering advertising reliable and inexpensive services, he planned the beginning of his conversation.

It was the varnish stain he'd found in the kidnappers' letter that had brought him here. Only three groups of people in Lower Limewood used varnish every day because of their trade. They were leather-workers, glaziers and carpenters, and Ambrosius expected to find Cody's kidnappers among them. He had already gone to see the leather-workers and the glaziers, and now he intended to visit the carpenters. He'd had no luck the day before, but perhaps a new day would bring a new clue?

He pushed open the door and purposefully stepped inside.

"Good morning!" he tipped his hat politely.

"Welcome, Inspector!" The master carpenter sprung up to greet him. "Please come in! How can I help you, Mr Nosegoode?"

Ambrosius swiftly surveyed the inside of the workshop. Piles of planks, pots of glue and paint, a set of tools hanging on the wall – none of these interested him much. What caught his attention was the master's apprentice, who was stubbornly smoothing down a wooden board with a plane. *Judging by his age*, Ambrosius thought, *he could be one of them.* From the outset, he had supposed that the kidnappers were young – that they were just embarking on the criminal path. His main reason for this assumption was the naive style of the letter. That's why his gaze lingered for a moment on the young man before he answered the master.

"You're wondering what brings me here," he said. "Well, it's a bit of a strange request. I would like... I would like to order a wooden scooter."

The master's jaw dropped open, and the apprentice with the plane froze for a moment and glanced at Mr Nosegoode with disapproval.

"Of course, I'm not planning to ride around on it myself! No, no," the detective explained with a grin. "It's supposed to be a gift for my godson, who's been dreaming about having a scooter. Would you be able to make me one?"

The master scratched his head.

"Hmm, that's got me a bit stumped," he replied. "I've made all sorts of things in my life, but nobody's ever asked me for a scooter. I could try, of course... But it might be better if you look around for a ready-made one. In fact, I recently saw one in Duckfield!"

"In Duckfield?"

"Yes. My cousin has a toy shop there, and that's where it was... Would you ever be going that way?"

"I have to think about it – I might make a little trip... In case I decide to go, can you give me the address of your cousin's shop?"

"Of course: it's 13 Nightingale Street."

Mr Nosegoode looked a bit flustered.

"I should write it down..." he said. "My memory isn't what it used to be... But I just realized I forgot my notebook." He turned to the apprentice. "Young man, could you do me a small favour and jot down the address for me?"

The assistant gave the master a questioning glance.

"What are you waiting for, Andy?" the latter said sharply. "Didn't you hear the inspector?"

Looking sheepish, the assistant quickly disappeared behind the heavy curtain separating one corner of the room from the rest of the workshop. He emerged a few seconds later holding a piece of paper and a pencil.

"All set," he announced. "Could you please repeat the address?"

The master repeated it, and Andy wrote it down slowly, sticking his tongue out to help with the task.

"Here you go, sir," he handed the piece of paper to Mr Nosegoode.

Reaching out for it, the detective observed the young man closely. He saw no indication of a guilty conscience: not a trace of fear or unease in his face, not a hint of a blush...

I don't think I've got the right person, he thought. *He looks like a good-natured chap, and his name begins with an A, not a G or a W.*

One glance at the piece of paper convinced him of Andy's innocence. His handwriting looked nothing like the letter-writer's. Of course, the letter about the meeting in Birch Grove could have been written by the other kidnapper, but Ambrosius's deep understanding of people – which rarely let him down – told him that Andy had nothing to do with Cody's disappearance.

He put the piece of paper in his pocket, thanked the master carpenter for his advice about the scooter and headed off to Swan Way.

He didn't stop there for long. On the door of the workshop, he found a brief but telling note. "Closed due to the carpenter's illness."

When he asked the caretaker of the building about the carpenter's apprentices or assistants, the latter eyed him suspiciously and declared that the last time he'd seen an apprentice in the workshop was when he still had thick, bushy curls. As he said this, he insolently rubbed his completely bald head.

There's only Barrel-Organ Street left! Ambrosius sighed inwardly and set off towards the last workshop. On the way, he wondered if he shouldn't invent a different excuse from the scooter, but in the end he decided against it. After all, talking about a scooter was much more amusing than talking about a hat stand, for example. *If only my godson, twirling his grey moustache somewhere, knew that I was looking for a scooter for him, he'd be splitting his sides laughing,* the detective thought as he entered the workshop, which belonged to Mr Titmouse.

"You're looking for a scooter?" Mr Titmouse lit up when Mr Nosegoode explained his request. "You've come to the right place! I'm not going to make one for you, but we'll get you a scooter for sure. Hey, boys!" he yelled to the two assistants who were busy assembling an enormous wardrobe. "Go to the storeroom and have a good poke around there; I'm sure there's something that will suit the inspector. No, wait! I'll come with you. If I let you in there on your own, you'll make such a mess that I'll need a whole year to work out what's where. Please excuse me, Inspector," he bowed to Mr Nosegoode. "It won't take long. Today's paper is on the shelf over there if you'd like to flick through it while you wait."

Having discharged this rapid stream of words, he put his arms around the two assistants and disappeared with them in the doorway leading to the storeroom.

Ambrosius decided not to waste a second. He swept the room with a keen glance. He stood up on his tiptoes, he crouched down, he looked more closely at a few things, and then at last he went up to the shelf with the newspaper. He reached for it – and froze. His heart bounced inside his chest like a little ball as he stared at a green notebook lying next to the newspaper.

The owner's name was written on the cover – it was George Warbler, and the letters G and W looked as if they'd been lifted straight out of the kidnappers' letter! Ambrosius had no doubt that it was the work of the same hand. *So the culprit must be here somewhere, in this workshop!* he thought, astonished by his discovery. *It must be one of Mr Titmouse's assistants! But which one? Or are both of them in it together?*

He glanced anxiously at the open door to the storeroom. Nobody: they were still searching, which meant he had a bit more time to come up with a plan.

I have to find out their names first, he thought. *I need to know which of them is George. But how to make them sing, without giving the game away?*

After a brief reflection, the detective's face lit up.

Just at that moment, Mr Titmouse appeared in the doorway, triumphantly brandishing a scooter.

"We've found one! Have a look! There's a bit of damage, but we can fix it up like new. Am I right, boys?"

The boys nodded eagerly and went back to putting the wardrobe together. That's exactly what Ambrosius had been waiting for.

"George..." he began loudly and broke off, observing the two assistants closely. "My godson George will love it, I'm sure," he finished in a quieter voice, clearly disappointed.

"No doubt!" Mr Titmouse agreed.

This little test demonstrated that there was no George present. If the owner of the green notebook had been in the room, he would surely have turned around when he heard his name. The assistants hadn't even budged. *Where is he*

then? Ambrosius wondered. *How can I find out?* He looked at the scooter and thought, *I can use this to help me!*

"So when can I pick it up?" he asked.

The master carpenter did some quick calculations in his head.

"Three days from now," he replied. "We need to finish this wardrobe first because the customer is getting impatient..."

"I see you've got a lot of work. You could use another assistant," the detective suggested slyly.

A shadow crossed the carpenter's face.

"I do have another one, but..." He waved his hand dismissively. "I hired him because his mother begged me to. She insisted on getting him trained as a carpenter, but learning the trade is the last thing on his mind. He comes here when he feels like it; he doesn't care... You see, he's not here again today."

"I think I might know this lazybones," Ambrosius ventured. "Isn't it that George from... from... Now, which street was it? Ah, my poor memory!"

"Brewery Street," Mr Titmouse said obligingly. "He lives at number eight. You know him, do you?"

"Well... not really, it's more his mother," the detective back-pedalled prudently. "She was telling me one day about her troubles with her son."

I shouldn't say too much, Ambrosius stopped himself, *because his partner in crime might be in the room.*

Just in case, he looked at the assistants to try to guess from their expressions what they thought of their co-worker. He could see such sincere disapproval in their faces – such complete agreement with the master's opinion of George – that he rejected the thought that one of them could be George's accomplice.

Reassured, he entrusted the scooter to Mr Titmouse and said goodbye. Swinging his cane gracefully, he stepped out into the street, which was bathed in May sunshine.

Cody, my dear friend! he thought with a surge of emotion. *Wherever you are, don't worry! The days of our separation are numbered!*

HELP, MR NOSEGOODE!

After leaving Mr Titmouse's workshop, Ambrosius headed straight to Brewery Street to take a look at the building where George Warbler lived. When he arrived, he was pleased to discover that the Sweet Corner café was directly across the road from number eight.

"A pretty good observation spot!" he said under his breath and went in.

The café was empty except for a young waitress, who was putting vases of fresh flowers on tables, rustling her freshly starched apron. Mr Nosegoode chose a seat by the window, ordered a hot chocolate and reached for *The Morning News*. Pretending to read, he kept peeking at the shabby building across the street. *It's not full of millionaires, that's for sure,* he thought, as he gazed at worn-out net curtains, a patched feather duvet airing out on a balcony and a bony cat soaking up the sun behind a windowpane. *As I sit here*, it occurred to Ambrosius, *George might be behind one of those windows. And maybe poor Cody is whimpering in the cellar or in some shed in the yard?*

At this last thought, Ambrosius felt a frantic desire to get up and check immediately, but he forced himself to stay calm. The many years of pursuing criminals had taught him that hurry was the biggest enemy of success.

He took a sip of his hot chocolate and, for the third time, began reading a short article about an exhibition of canaries. But his eyes kept flitting to the side, and he never did manage to finish the article. Something flashed in the doorway across the street and... Ambrosius almost dropped his paper. *That could be him! Yes, that must be him!* A slim youth emerged from the doorway, stood with his legs wide apart, spat on the ground and stared at a farmer's cart wobbling over the cobblestones. *It's him!* Ambrosius thought again and looked at the waitress, as though he wanted her to confirm his guess. The waitress met his gaze and stopped what she was doing.

"Excuse me, miss," Ambrosius began. "That young man standing in front of the door across the street... is that... Charlie Catlow?" he blurted out the first name that popped into his head.

The waitress went up to the window, parted the net curtains and shook her head.

"I don't know Charlie Catlow, sir," she replied. "But that certainly isn't Charlie."

"Oh!" Ambrosius pretended to be surprised. "How can you be so sure?"

"Because that's George Warbler. And if it's George, it can't be Charlie, can it?" She laughed, amused by her own answer.

Ambrosius smiled in return.

"I asked about Charlie," he continued genially, "because I was told that he had gone to visit a friend of his at number eight. I don't know him, you see, but there's something I'd like to talk to him about. Maybe this George here is the friend he's come to see. Do you know who his friends are by any chance?"

"I don't know them all – how would I? But George often hangs out with a fellow named Bertie Chubb."

"Ah, never mind," Ambrosius seemed to ignore her last words. "I'll manage. Thank you for your help!"

"No problem," the waitress said and went back to her flowers.

The detective shifted his gaze to George, who stretched, yawned and set off in the direction of the main square. Ambrosius waited a couple of minutes before paying the bill and leaving the café.

Out on the street, he hesitated, wondering what to do: follow George and possibly find out who his partner in crime was, or explore the building to look for Cody? After thinking it over briefly, he crossed the road to number eight and stepped through the dim entrance. It was cool inside, and the air was filled with the smell of sauerkraut. *I'll start with the courtyard*, he decided as he opened the door opposite the entrance.

Clearing his throat from time to time, Ambrosius walked back and forth past the small windows of the cellar and lingered for a while by a little shed that stood in one corner – but there was no response, no other sound of any kind. The conclusion was clear: Cody wasn't being held prisoner in either the shed or the cellar. Otherwise he would have sensed the detective's presence and made some sort of sound.

That left only two other places where Cody could be. in George's flat or in the attic. Ambrosius went back inside, found the Warblers' name on the list of tenants and began climbing up to the third floor, where they lived. He paused in front of their door, coughed and listened for a while – again, there was no sound. The result was exactly the same up in the attic.

He's not in the building, Ambrosius concluded with regret. *They must have taken him somewhere else. But where? Perhaps he's at the other kidnapper's.* Contemplating this, he walked slowly back to Skylark Lane.

When he turned into his street, he saw Francis Nailer, the retired postal clerk with whom he sometimes played bridge, pacing nervously back and forth in front of number seven. Ambrosius quickened his steps: he knew that this sort of pacing was not a good sign.

He wasn't mistaken. One glance at Mr Nailer's face was enough to know that he hadn't come to play cards. His brow was furrowed, and his eyes were full of anguish.

"Help, Mr Nosegoode!" the visitor exclaimed when the detective got nearer.

"What's the matter, Mr Nailer?" Ambrosius asked with surprise.

Francis Nailer looked around anxiously, then pulled a crumpled envelope out of his pocket and handed it to Mr Nosegoode.

Inside was a small sheet of paper on which was written:

Dear Sir! Listen. Your pigeons are in danger. Someone wants to poisen them. We can save them, but you have to pay us five hundred pounds. Please get the money ready and wait for the next letter. We will write to tell you where to leeve the money. If you report this to the police or tell anyone, that's the end of your pigeons.

Hooknose and Cinnamon

Mr Nailer eyed Ambrosius carefully as he read the letter. When the detective finished, he asked, "Do you understand now?"

Ambrosius understood perfectly. The pigeons were Mr Nailer's greatest passion! He had devoted half his life to them. He took great pride in them, loved them and cared for them as if they were his own children – the children he'd never had. And now they were in mortal danger.

Ambrosius read the letter again. The handwriting looked nothing like the writing in the letter about Birch Grove. There were fewer errors too. But that signature: Hooknose and Cinnamon... Why did those nicknames seem so familiar? He was sure he'd come across them before – but where? He *had* to remember. He focused all his mental energies... Where was it? He concentrated his thoughts... Yes, that was it! It was all crystal clear now!

Francis Nailer watched the detective with increasing concern. Why did he look so animated all of a sudden? And so happy? Didn't he get it?

"Mr Nosegoode," he began. "Please help me. I can't go to the police because they might follow me. I've come to you because I trust you. Please don't ignore this letter..."

"I'm not going to ignore it!" Ambrosius reassured him wholeheartedly. "And I understand perfectly. If I'm in high spirits, it's because Hooknose and Cinnamon are nearly within my grasp and your pigeons are safe. I mean it!"

"But... but... but how can that be?" Mr Nailer stuttered. "How could you... so quickly..."

Ambrosius was genuinely amused.

"My name is Nosegoode, Mr Nailer. And that means something! You can go home without a worry and wait for

the next letter from these scoundrels. That's when we'll make our move. And I'm hoping we won't be alone. If my suspicions are correct, we should have a helper. I'll see you soon! I have to dash off to the library because that's where I expect to find the last link in the logical chain I've been piecing together over the past few days."

He hurried off briskly, leaving Mr Nailer baffled but reassured.

The local librarian, Mrs Sophie Sage, knew Mr Nosegoode well and she greeted him cheerfully.

"I'm so glad you've come, Mr Nosegoode! I have something for you!"

She sprang up from her desk, ran over to a bookshelf and came back holding a copy of *Portraits of Extraordinary Dogs*.

"Look! I bought this yesterday. There's an entry in here about you and your dog. There's even a photo of him! Have you seen it?"

"I've not only seen it; I've bought a copy," Ambrosius replied, although he had the distinct impression that Mrs Sage would have preferred a negative answer.

"Ah, pity!" the librarian sighed. "I thought it would be a nice surprise..."

"Every book you lend me is a nice surprise," Ambrosius consoled her.

She thanked him with a smile and asked what he was after.

"Today I'm looking for something related to my old line of work," he said. "Do you have a copy of a novel by Onuphrius Angel titled *The Black Dog, or the Mystery of Old Shuck's Cove?*"

"Yes, I'm sure we do, but I think someone might have borrowed it. Let me check."

She bent over the card index, flipped through a few cards and held up her hands in apology.

"I'm sorry, but it's on loan at the moment."

"What bad luck!" Ambrosius pretended to be disappointed. "I wonder who snatched it from under my nose."

The librarian bent her head down again.

"Let's see." It took only a few swift flicks of her fingers before she had the answer. "It's Mrs Chubb."

"Ah, yes... The one who lives in Lapwing Lane?" Ambrosius asked, even though he didn't know a Mrs Chubb, never mind one in Lapwing Lane.

"No, the one in Station Street."

Ambrosius had no further questions. He had an old friend in Station Street, the owner of a second-hand bookshop, and he reckoned he would be able to find out more from him about Mrs Chubb and, more importantly, about Bertie Chubb.

He wasn't disappointed. After briefly explaining everything to his friend, he learned that Mrs Chubb was an elderly lady who lived with her two dogs, a cat and a nephew. While her four-legged friends didn't cause her much trouble, her nephew made up for it in spades. Instead of helping his aunt to make artificial flowers – her only means of income – the boy sat about all day doing nothing or hanging around with shady characters.

"Not too long ago," the bookseller continued, "he even turned up here, in my shop, in the company of one of his pals, and asked about some detective novel. Wait, what was the title?"

"*The Black Dog, or the Mystery of Old Shuck's Cove,*" Ambrosius offered.

"That's it! How did you know?" his friend was amazed.

"Because that book plays a key role in the whole affair," Ambrosius explained. "Bertie and the other chap must have

read his aunt's library copy and then wanted to buy one for their own purposes. That's why they came here."

"I see that the famous Detective Nosegoode from the old days is still alive and well!" the bookseller said with appreciation. "Are you sure you haven't retired too early?"

Ambrosius dismissed the question with a wistful smile. "Don't tease me," he said.

Their conversation moved on to other topics, such as the weather, politics and their health. Ambrosius, whose mood had been somewhat dampened by his friend's question, quickly regained his good humour. After all, he had found what he'd been looking for: the last link in his chain!

A CONVERSATION WITH THE MILLER'S GHOST

The clock on the wall made a grinding sound, its little doors opened with a bang and the cuckoo burst out and cuckooed eleven times. Ambrosius twitched in his armchair so abruptly that the springs squeaked. He blinked. *I've dozed off*, he realized with surprise. He had just wanted a little rest after the day's unusual adventures, but instead he had fallen asleep.

The day had been unusual indeed: several mysteries had been solved. Ambrosius now knew for sure who had written the letter about the meeting in Birch Grove, and he had also learned the name of the accomplice and the reason for Cody's kidnapping. The only thing he didn't know was where to find Cody, but he hoped to learn that soon.

He got up from the armchair, walked over to his sofa bed and started preparing it for the night. He was laying out the duvet when he heard an urgent banging on the front door. He froze for a moment in anticipation. When the banging started again, he walked over to the door.

"Who's there?" he enquired.

"It's me," a panting, unfamiliar voice said. "I'm a foot cream salesman. Are you Mr Ambrosius Nosegoode?"

"Yes, I am," Ambrosius replied. "But I'm afraid you've got the wrong person. As luck would have it, my feet are in fine shape. Do you have anything for hair loss?"

"Please don't joke like that!" the voice behind the door said imploringly. "I haven't come here to talk business."

"Then what have you come to talk about?"

A brief silence was followed by an embarrassed whisper. "Ghosts..."

"What?!"

"Ghosts," came the even quieter answer.

Ambrosius put his face against the door and asked, also in a whisper, "My dear sir... Please tell me – in all honesty – what have you been drinking today?"

"Only milk," the foot-cream salesman replied. "Goat's milk," he added, to dispel any doubts.

"Are you sure?" Ambrosius wasn't convinced.

"Absolutely! As sure as I am of the fact that my foot

cream is the best cure for callouses and cracked heels. But I can explain everything, if you please let me in!"

Amused by this unusual visit, the detective shrugged to himself and unlocked the door.

"Please do come in."

A short, slim man with a frightened expression and darting eyes stepped inside, carrying a small suitcase plastered with colourful stickers. He was smartly dressed and his large polka-dot bowtie, which bounced up and down comically as he spoke, added to his overall elegance. Without waiting for an invitation, he sank into a chair, pulled a handkerchief out of his pocket and started to wipe his forehead. Once he'd had time to calm down, he spoke again.

"Mr Nosegoode, do you believe in ghosts?"

Ambrosius assumed a serious expression, appropriate to the gravity of the question.

"No, I don't," he declared. "But I'm a bit afraid of them."

"Huh?"

"Well, you see," he continued, "I don't believe in them either, but they might not know that..."

"You're having fun at my expense again," the ointment salesman said indignantly. "But I'm being completely serious. I've met a ghost!"

The detective's patience was beginning to run out.

"Where?" he asked dryly.

"By the Old Mill."

"And what did this ghost look like?"

The man seemed thrown by this question.

"I didn't see him. I only heard him."

"So how do you know it was a ghost?"

"Because he introduced himself. He said, 'Halt, kind stranger, and listen to me! I'm the old miller's ghost! I have some urgent business for Ambrosius Nosegoode, who lives in Lower Limewood, in Skylark Lane. Could you do me a favour?' This is what he said, so I stopped and listened."

In an instant, Ambrosius seemed completely transformed. His eyes lit up. He grabbed the salesman by the shoulder and shook him, crying out, "My good man! Tell me everything, starting from the very beginning! In the right order and with all the details!"

The salesman was momentarily alarmed but quickly regained his composure. Pleased by his host's unexpected interest, he began his tale.

"I was in a nearby village when nightfall caught me by surprise. There was nowhere to spend the night out there, so I was hurrying to a hotel in Lower Limewood. I wanted to get to bed as soon as possible, so I took a shortcut – a shortcut that leads by the Old Mill. Of course, I'd heard stories about how the mill was haunted, but I'd laughed them off, like any sensible person. I have to confess that as I got closer to the old ruin, I felt a bit ill at ease, but I told myself to be sensible and picked up my pace. Just as I was walking past the building, I heard what sounded like a bark – and then the words you've just heard. You can't imagine what it was like! I was petrified. My legs felt rooted to the spot. I couldn't move them at all, no matter how hard I tried. Meanwhile, that hollow, gloomy voice continued: 'Go and tell Ambrosius Nosegoode that I have an important secret to share with him. If he wants to learn what it is, he must come here, to the Old Mill, at midnight tonight. Will do you me this small favour, kind stranger?' What was I supposed to do? I promised I would, though my throat was so tight I could hardly get a word out. The hollow voice thanked me and assured me that I'd be remembered in the other world. I finally regained control of my legs and ran all the way here."

He finished speaking and stared at Ambrosius, waiting for his reaction.

Ambrosius said simply, "All right! I'll be there at midnight."

Then he put a bottle of blackcurrant wine on the table and cleverly changed the topic of conversation to the other adventures which his genial guest must have undoubtedly had during his years of travelling.

They said their goodbyes when the cuckoo clock showed eleven thirty-five. Ambrosius saw his visitor to the door and waited a few minutes before grabbing his cane and a torch and setting off to meet the ghost.

I'm going to be late, he thought as he walked, *but I hope that the ghost – who exists outside of time, after all – is not going to be too upset about a quarter of an hour's delay.*

It was well after midnight when he finally found himself in front of the dark hulk of the windmill. He had to wait a while for his heart to stop pounding madly after the brisk march.

At last, he took a few steps forward and called out, "Cody! My friend! I'm here!"

Something inside the mill shifted abruptly, and Ambrosius heard the familiar voice, although it sounded a bit different because it was so full of emotion.

"Ambrosius! Ambrosius!"

They rejoiced at finally finding each other, and it took a few seconds before Cody could speak again.

"Come inside!" he said. "The door is bolted from the outside. I have so much to tell you!"

Elated, Ambrosius rushed up the steps to the door, quickly opened the bolt, burst inside – and the two friends embraced each other at last.

Once their joyful whoops had died down, Cody briefly described what had happened to him since he'd been kidnapped, and Ambrosius told him how he'd tracked down George Warbler and Bertie Chubb.

When his friend came to the end, Cody said, "Do you know what these louts have in mind for me? Do you know why they've kidnapped me?"

"Of course," Ambrosius replied.

"Really?!"

Ambrosius rarely managed to surprise his dog, so this outburst of disbelief and admiration pleased him immensely.

"Really," he said. "You've been kidnapped so that, after suitable training, you can pick up the ransom which the kidnappers are planning to collect. Am I right?"

"You are!" Cody replied in astonishment. "But how did you work it out?"

Ambrosius waited a moment before replying, to arouse Cody's curiosity even more. Then he said, "I didn't have much working out to do. They put me on the right track themselves."

"What do you mean? You've actually talked to them?"

"Oh no, they haven't yet had that pleasure!" Ambrosius exclaimed. "But your caring guardians have had time to write a threatening letter, demanding a ransom. And they signed that letter with nicknames taken from a certain book..."

"I think I know what they are!" the dog interrupted. "Hooknose and Cinnamon!"

It was the detective's turn to be surprised.

"But how do you know about that? Were you there when they wrote the letter?"

Cody realized that the moment of his own triumph had come.

"No," he began, pausing even longer before continuing slowly, drawing out each word. "But I've also read Onuphrius Angel's novel, and sometimes I put my dog brain to good use. So when my 'caring guardians' – as you've decided to call them – took me outside for the first time and ordered me to fetch a package from under a tree, I immediately remembered *The Black Dog, or the Mystery of Old Shuck's Cove.* Cinnamon and Hooknose, the protagonists of that book, used exactly the same method to train their dog to fetch them the ransom left by innocent, frightened people in the appointed spot. It wasn't hard to guess that these two were preparing me for a similar role."

"In other words," Ambrosius summed things up, "Onuphrius Angel helped both of us. Let's be grateful to him for that! Do you have any other questions?"

"Yes, just one. Who did my 'caring guardians' write to with their ransom demand? Who's supposed to be their next victim?"

"Francis Nailer, the owner of the finest flock of pigeons for miles around. They told him that his pigeons would be poisoned if he didn't hand over five hundred pounds."

"Scoundrels!" Cody was beside himself with outrage. "Do you think they'd carry out their threat?"

"I have no idea. I don't know them well enough."

"They might think twice about that..." the dog reasoned out loud. "But in any case, we won't let them go through with it, will we? What are you planning to do next?"

"I'll wait for the second letter from Cinnamon and Hooknose, or rather George and Bertie – or Spotty and Barrel, as you've dubbed them. Then I'll put a little package of my own in the appointed spot and catch them in the act. Do you approve of the plan?"

"I do. We just need to discuss a few details. But before that, I've thought of another question."

"Yes?"

"Ambrosius," the dog began, and his voice suddenly sounded very soft. "Tell me, did you worry about me much?"

"Not much," came the harsh answer.

Cody's heart sank in his chest.

"I didn't worry much," Ambrosius continued, "because I know that when someone kidnaps a brilliant dog, it's not to do him harm. On top of that, I believe in you. And do you think I would ever let anyone hurt you?"

Cody smiled to himself.

"There's something I've been trying to work out for a long time," he said, gazing into a dark corner of the room.

"What is it?"

"Which part of your personality is stronger: your attachment to me or your pride in your own abilities? I have to say I'm asking myself this very question right now."

"How interesting!" Ambrosius picked up his tone. "Because I often ask myself this same question. About you, of course!"

The two friends looked at each other and burst into loud, carefree laughter.

A DRAMATIC NIGHT AT THE OLD MILL

It was dark and quiet inside the mill. Only now and then, when a stronger gust of wind struck the wooden ruin, a plank would creak somewhere, a beam would groan, or something would come splatting down onto the floor... Spotty and Barrel, meaning George Warbler and Bertie Chubb, hadn't lit the candle on top of the millstone. They were worried that the light might filter out through the cracks in the walls and betray their presence. So they remained in the dark, with their heads squeezed close together in front of a little window and their eyes fixed on the lone poplar tree looming in the distance.

It was nearly ten, the time when Francis Nailer was supposed to lay a package containing five hundred pounds under the tree. Tension was mounting. The boys broke the silence only now and then, speaking in clipped, anxious sentences. Only Cody was calm, lying curled up in a ball and waiting for his cue to enter the game.

"What's the time?" Bertie whispered.

George raised his arm up to his eyes.

"Five to."

"You think he'll be on time?"

"I'm not thinking. I'm waiting."

"What if he doesn't show up?"

"He will show up."

Another gust of wind made the building shake, and at that moment the boys heard a stifled sneeze. They froze.

"What was that?" Bertie said with an effort.

"I don't know. Maybe the dog."

They looked at Cody, who quickly moved his head and snorted, trying to imitate the sound, which he had also heard.

"Phew, the dog..." they sighed in relief and resumed their watch.

"If he comes much later," Bertie began, "it's going to be so dark we won't be able to see a thing."

"Don't say that!" George snapped. "You forgot about the moon."

As if to confirm his words, the golden disc of the moon emerged from behind clouds and dispelled some of the darkness.

They were silent for a time.

"My eyes are hurting from all this staring," Bertie spoke again.

"So stop staring," George advised him.

Bertie closed his eyelids for a few seconds, and just at that moment he heard George's stifled cry.

"He's coming!"

He instantly opened his eyes. After staring into the darkness for a few moments, he could make out a figure walking slowly towards the poplar. Judging by his height, it was Francis Nailer.

"There he is!" he said in a muffled voice.

They both fell silent again, keeping their eyes fixed on the indistinct figure walking through the field. Their breathing grew faster and louder. The figure approached the tree, paused, looked all around and then leaned down, as if to lay something on the ground.

"He's brought it!" Bertie blurted out.

"I told you he would," George reminded him in a boastful tone.

They focused all their attention on Francis Nailer. Having done what he came to do, he quickly strode off in the direction of Lower Limewood.

"Was he alone for sure?" Bertie asked.

"You saw for yourself!"

Bertie nodded. He glanced at the dog and added, "We can let him out now."

"Wait a bit! It doesn't hurt to be extra careful."

They watched the area around the poplar for a while. When nothing suspicious happened, George decided that it was time.

"Let's make a start!"

They left their post by the window and quickly led Cody to the exit, stumbling over bits of clutter on the floor. They were much more nervous than during the practice sessions. No wonder: it wasn't a packet of pigeon thighs lying under the poplar now!

Outside the mill, they breathed deeply, surveyed the surroundings once more and gestured to each other that everything was fine. George laid a hand on the dog's back. His hand was shaking – just like his voice when he said, "Well, Cody, show us what you can do! Fetch!"

The dog understood instantly what was required and without needing further encouragement leapt into the darkness.

"He obeyed!..." The two boys heaved a sigh of relief and the weight of doubt was lifted from their shoulders. Up until that moment, they had been worried the dog might have an unpleasant surprise for them.

Luckily, he didn't. Cody ran straight ahead, and they watched him, urging him along in their minds and feeling panic whenever he disappeared from view. The seconds seemed to drag on for ever...

The dog was a third of the way there now, and it was harder and harder to make him out in the dim light. He kept melting into the background, until he finally disappeared for good as the clouds closed over the moon. The suspense was unbearable. Was he still running towards the tree? Would he pick up the package? Would he bring it back?

They muttered to each other about their misgivings and tried to peer through the veil of darkness that obscured the field, but it was no good. They could see very little beyond the bright spots flickering in front of their eyes... Even the poplar tree was barely visible.

All of a sudden – was it one minute later or fifteen? – the moon came out again, casting a faint light, and...

"He's coming back!" they cried out almost exactly in the same instant.

Sure enough, a small shadow was rapidly moving towards them through the field. Cody! Cody! Their throats were dry from excitement, and they couldn't help themselves. They started running towards the dog, to make sure that he hadn't let them down.

*

They reach Cody quickly, grab the flat package out of his mouth and start running frantically back to the mill, forgetting completely about the dog, who follows them with a disdainful smile.

They burst inside, bend over the millstone and start groping for matches, but one match after another breaks and they can't get the candle lit – until at last a small flame illuminates the room. George grabs the package, stares at it intently as if he were hoping to see through the brown paper, and then with a quick motion rips it open and... what on earth?! His eyes grow wider and wider.

He snarls, "Look! Look how the old geezer has stitched us up!"

He shakes the paper wrapping and out of it tumble four plump sausages.

"Look what he's brought us!" he adds through clenched teeth.

In the same instant, a bright torch beam cuts through the gloom and a booming voice rings out, "It's not for you, my dear friends, not for you! The sausages are for the dog. This is what we have for you!"

*

The two boys jumped up in alarm and saw Constable Longbeak emerge out of the storeroom holding two pairs of handcuffs. Behind him was Ambrosius Nosegoode. The whole windmill seemed to spin. Escape was impossible, even if their legs didn't refuse to obey them. They stood silently rooted to the spot, with their eyes fixed on the millstone, and waited. Constable Longbeak put the handcuffs in his pocket, walked over to the two of them, grabbed them by their collars and pushed them towards the door. They obeyed, meek as lambs.

It was only then that Ambrosius ran up to Cody, knelt down, took the dog's head in his hands, looked into the faithful eyes and said, "Our separation is over, my friend! Time to go home!"

Cody affectionately brushed against Ambrosius's knee. Then he smiled mischievously and said, "Happily, but not straight away."

"Why not?"

"Because I still have something important to do here."

"And that is?"

"I need to check if those sausages taste as good as they look!" Cody replied, licking his lips.

We created Pushkin Children's Books to share tales from different languages and cultures with younger readers, and to open the door to the wide, colourful worlds these stories offer.

From picture books and adventure stories to fairy tales and classics, and from fifty-year-old bestsellers to current huge successes abroad, the books on the Pushkin Children's list reflect the very best stories from around the world, for our most discerning readers of all: children.